JUST US KIDS - SHIPWRECKED

D. STEWART

Print Version:

ISBN-13:978-1547109289

ISBN-10:1547109289

Written by: D. Stewart

Illustrated by: Micaela Stéfano
http://kaleidoscopicdesign.tumblr.com

✿ Created with Vellum

DEDICATION

To the hard working writers in Mrs. Richardson's 4th grade class, who were the best Beta readers ever. Your notes and feedback helped shape this story. Keep writing! Your futures are bright, your dreams are achievable, and your writing will take you places!

Thank you:

Mrs. Richardson, Jordyn, Clara, Dessiree, Bryan, Jaden, Daniel, Cruz, Damarieon, Hunter, Abbie, Pennie, Julia, Dylan, Kamiyah, Victori, Isabell, Angel, Jordan, Landyn, Hannah, Arrianna, Zach, Annabel

JUST US KIDS - SHIPWRECKED

Tyler Hartmann had made mistakes, but today was the worst so far. The ship he was on with his mom had been caught in a storm and slammed against some rocks. Soaked by the pouring rain and confused by the darkness, Tyler and the other children had jumped into a lifeboat. It was what they'd been taught by the captain their first day on the ship. But the adults had all gotten on a separate lifeboat. When the two crafts hit the water and were battered by the waves, there had been no way to keep them together.

We are on our own. Just Us Kids

CHAPTER ONE

"I want my mom," the youngest boy finally says through his little cries when the sun comes up. At least it isn't dark anymore.

"It's all right," Rory says and I almost believe her. She's the only other kid I know out of this bunch. We hung out some during the first ten days of this voyage. That was before everything went wrong. Rory is close to my age. She's ten and I'm eleven. The three other kids are younger. Probably seven or eight. I notice the younger you are the more scared you get when things happen.

"Don't tell him that," another little boy cries. "You don't know if we are all right. We're lost at sea and alone. We don't have anything we need."

Everyone is looking at me and waiting for me to tell them what to do. Even Rory is. I guess being the oldest means you're in charge.

"Rory is right," I say, having to clear my dry throat. "We are going to be fine. I'm Tyler. What are your names?"

"Willie," the youngest crying boy says.

"Tom," the cranky boy answers.

"Julie," the quiet little girl holding a doll says.

"We're going to be fine," I tell them and hope they believe me. This is what you're supposed to do for little kids. If we are going to get out of this, I know for sure crying won't help. "We need to figure out what we have for supplies: food, water, a way to communicate."

"I have two bottles of water," Rory says, pulling them out of her pink bag with a silly unicorn on the front. When I first saw it back on the main ship I thought the bag was ugly. Now I'm happy to see it. Any supplies we have are better than none.

"I have a granola bar," Willie says with a little whistle when he speaks from his missing front teeth. "My mom always puts snacks in my pocket. I'm so hungry."

"We can't eat or drink any of it yet." I'm no expert but I know my stuff better than most kids. I've done wilderness training for the last four summers, and this trip to Australia is my dream come true. I'm ready for an adventure. Just not without any adults. That's not part of the plan.

My mom and I flew to England and boarded the Odin, the ship that would take us on the long journey to Australia. It was beautiful and sailed smoothly through the first part of the trip. I wish we were back on the Odin right now instead of the small lifeboat bobbing at sea.

"I'm so thirsty," Willie complains, his red hair so bright it's the same color as the rising sun. His freckles are glowing bright and his skin looks like it will burn easily if we don't get him some sunscreen.

"What else do we have?" Rory asks, pointing to my bag.

I list out what I have in my survival kit:

- 8-Hour Light Stick
- Box of Waterproof Matches
- 12 Emergency Drinking Water Pouches
- Multi-tool Survival Knife

- Survival Whistles
- 50 Ft All Purpose Utility Rope

I felt silly having all this stuff in my pack earlier, but now I am glad. Better safe than sorry. That's what all the guide books tell you.

"But what about food?" Julie asks, whimpering because her stomach is rumbling. I'm hungry too, but I know it's not the most important problem we have right now.

"You can live up to three weeks without food," I explain, not thinking how dumb I'm being. Little kids can't think about things like that without getting scared.

"I don't want to be that hungry," Julie moans. "Three weeks?"

I try to make her feel better. "You should be more concerned about water. You can only live three or four days without water. That's our real problem."

All three kids start crying, and my stomach turns from hungry to flip flopping with worry. Man, I am not good with little kids.

"We have water, and we're going to get food," Rory says, walking on the wobbly boat and crouching down in front of them. "I promise."

I want to tell Rory that she can't promise that, but somehow the little kids stop crying and that's more important than arguing about who is right or wrong.

"What can we eat?" Julie asks, looking around the small lifeboat.

"This is my granola bar," Willie says holding it close to him and pouting.

"Everything belongs to all of us now," I say, standing up and trying to balance. "The only way we're going to survive this is together. We have to be a team."

"Do you know what to do?" Tom asks. His cheeks still had

3

tears on them. His face is round and his cheeks are as pudgy as a chipmunk's. I saw him once on the Odin, and I know he had glasses, but they probably fell off in the storm.

I look at Rory, who is making a weird face at me. It's like she's telling me I better say yes. Even if the answer is no.

"Of course," I answer, puffing up my chest and trying to look bigger than I am. "I know exactly what to do."

END OF CHAPTER 1 STATS

Achievement: 1017 words!

Characters:
Tyler 11 years old
Rory 10 years old
Tom 7 years old
Willie 7 years old
Julie 6 years old

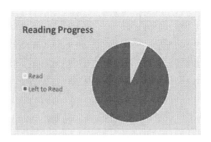

CHAPTER 2

The last few drops of water are hanging out at the bottom of my canteen when we first see the island.

Rory and I jump off the lifeboat and start to swim with the waves toward the shore. We hold on to the straps of the lifeboat and pull it along with us. Finding this island is a relief because I was about to tell everyone when we ran out of fresh drinking water our next option would be drinking turtle blood. Not very appetizing, and I know the kids would start crying again.

"Do you think there are sharks?" Rory asks out of breath as we pull the boat closer to the shore. I feel smooth rocks under my feet, and I can stand rather than swim. We still pull the lifeboat behind us, but it's easier now that I'm standing.

"Of course," I answer because I know this water is warm enough for sharks and full of food for them. This water would be perfect for all kinds of scary things.

"You need to stop that," Rory says, swimming faster. She's not as tall as I am, and her feet don't touch the bottom yet. "Just say there are no sharks here."

"I tell the truth," I answer, but I move a little faster too. Becoming shark food sounds like a terrible way to start this new day.

The sand is under our feet now, and we can both stand. We practically run the boat onto the shore.

The kids are cheering as they tumble out of the lifeboat they have been in for two days. I start trying to figure out right away what I can about the island. But the kids, even Rory, are just rolling around in the sand like everything will be okay now. *I'm not supposed to tell them they are wrong.*

"We need to find out if there is fresh water here," I remind them. It seems like they keep forgetting no one is here to help us. It's just us kids, and if we need something it's up to us to get it.

"I need to rest," Rory whines, flopping on her back. "We all do."

"No." I put my hands on my hips and look at all of them acting ridiculous. I feel like my teacher, Mrs. Richardson. She always makes sure our class does what we're supposed to, even when we feel like flopping around and doing nothing. I now realize she has a hard job. "There is no time. The good news is there are plenty of coconut trees and palms. That means there is probably fresh water. Maybe even people."

"I wonder what island this is," Rory says, staring at the sky. "I wonder where we are."

"I hope my dad is all right," Tom says, not rolling in the sand anymore. His face looks sad and worried. His eyebrows kind of wrinkle together.

"They are," Rory says. "For sure. They probably just drifted a different way. Or they already were picked up by a rescue boat, and they are looking for us."

"Or they don't have any supplies, and they are not okay," Willie says, pouting.

Rory is angry when she answers, and it makes my stomach jump with worry. "My dad is the best survival guide in the United

States," she explains. "He wrote the books that made all of you want to come with us to Australia."

"Your dad is Mickey Loots?" Tom asks with wide excited eyes.

"Yes," Rory answers, now looking embarrassed. Her cheeks are pink, and she looks away from all of us.

"I've read all his books," I say, thinking of the hours I spent in my room trying to imagine the adventures I could have someday. His books were my favorite. Now that I'm on an adventure, it's funny because I just want to go home.

"Where do we go to the bathroom? Like number two?" Willie asks, looking around like a toilet might grow out of the sand if he looked long enough.

We all laugh because no matter where you are that is funny. "Dig a hole," I tell him, pointing into the woods. "Find some soft leaves because there is no toilet paper here."

"He can't just go in the woods," Rory corrects, and now she sounds like the leader. "We don't know what's out there."

She's right. This is a completely unknown place. I know what could be here though, and it's not good. The list is endless. First there are the small insects and spiders to worry about. From creepy crawlies to the long and slithering poisonous snakes that could be anywhere from the trees to the ground.

I need to find a place for shelter and a bathroom for this group. We need to stay far away from the poisonous trees and brush, but we need cover from the sun. This seemed easier when it was something I was reading in a book.

"Willie, give me a second. I'm going to check out the area to the left of that large overhanging tree." They all stare at me as if maybe I won't come back. Maybe something out there will get me, and they'll be on their own.

"Okay, but make it quick, Tyler." Willie makes a face like he can't hold it much longer.

When I get to the area, it looks fairly safe and private. I check out the ground for something to dig with. There's a piece of bark that should do the trick. After inspecting it for spiders, I pick it up. It takes me a few minutes, but I dig a small hole. I'm sweating right through my T-shirt because the sun feels so hot.

"Almost ready for me, Tyler?" Willie asks, squirming over to me.

"That is your bathroom," I explain and Willie looks puzzled then it clicks.

"I don't really like it here," Willie complains.

"Me either," I say, walking away to explore some more.

Having a quiet moment to myself I think about everyone else who was on that ship with us. I hope they are okay. Is my mom worried? She always worries. I stare out at the horizon over the ocean. It's beautiful. This island is too. I almost forget for a minute to be scared. *Almost.*

END OF CHAPTER 2 STATS

<u>Achievement:</u> 2122 words!

<u>Characters:</u>
   Tyler - Prepared
   Rory - Brave
   Tom - Worried
   Willie - Nervous
   Julie- Hungry

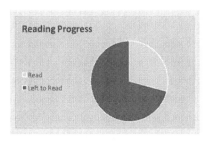

CHAPTER 3

"Rory, if I had to be stuck on an island with any kid, I would want it to be you. We should be able to put our heads together and come up with a plan," I say as we keep working to get things set up.

"I hope you are right, Tyler," Rory says, sounding tired.

"Julie, you are six, right?" I ask, amazed at how much energy Julie has.

"Yes." She sounds proud, and I remember how I used to get excited every time I became a year older.

"Why don't you help Rory draw out the letters S.O.S in the sand?" I instruct, talking to her like I would any little kid. Julie jumps to her feet and runs to Rory's side, ready to help. Everyone, no matter how young, has to help out.

"Willie and I will grab leaves and palm ferns to fill in the letters you draw in the sand so they stand out more. We need someone to watch for a rescue plane flying over." I try to sound excited.

Too afraid to venture into the jungle any farther than I have already, I stay around the outside, where I can still see the others. We gather enough palms to fill where Julie and Rory made a large S.O.S sign. I have no clue if it's as big as it should be to get the attention of a plane, but I'm too tired to tell them to make it bigger. Tommy didn't know what it meant, so Rory explained it meant Save Our Ship. Which only led to a lot more questions about how we aren't even on a ship. And maybe it should be S.O.B.—save our butts. Rory finally gave up and admitted she didn't know why you were supposed to do S.O.S.—she just knew you were supposed to.

Once that is complete I go back to the edge of the woods to gather sticks for a fire. Fire is an important part of survival. Twigs and small logs are stacked up in my arms.

"Tom, I need your help," I yell as I start to fumble the wood.

"Um, okay, Tyler," Tom says, looking nervous.

"I'm going to try and get a fire going. We need it to stay warm and dry and boil water if we find some. Help me bring these over."

Tom moves too fast and tries to snatch up the whole pile from my arms. A large splinter sticks him.

"Ouch!" he exclaims, dropping the pile on both our feet.

"Are you okay?" I ask, and I see Tom's neck move as he swallows really hard.

"My mommy always used a Band-Aid and a kiss to make my boo-boos better." The tears flow from Tom's eyes, and I'm not sure if it's because he misses his mom or the splinter really hurts.

"I have to take that splinter out of your palm," I tell him. "Then we should rinse it in the salt water."

"Will it hurt?" Tom asks, closing his eyes tight and sticking his hand out for me to help.

"It's not so bad," I tell him and feel sick when I see the splinter and a little blood around it. I take hold of the thick splinter and yank it out all at once. After we rinse it in salt water, I rip some fabric off my shirt and tie it around his hand. I can't believe how brave he is. When I first saw these little kids on the lifeboat with me I was sure they'd spend all their time crying. But Tom is acting tough.

"We should start the fire, right?" Tom asks, leaning down to pick up the fallen wood. I call Rory over to help.

Rory hands me the waterproof matches. I'm so glad I packed them. I could probably rub two sticks together and make a spark after a while, but my arms are already so tired I'll use the matches. The wood is placed just like the survival book describes. The flame starts slow but eventually takes hold, and I realize I've built a fire. A real fire. Just like in the book.

"Now we need to keep this fire going. Got it team?" I ask. They all nod but look concerned. "It's important we keep this going for a few reasons."

"Rory, take Tom and gather all the twigs, branches, and logs you can find. Let's make a big pile. Watch what you are grabbing and pay attention to what's around you. You know what to be careful of."

"I sure do; my Dad taught me well," Rory says with confidence. "Sometimes it's all we talk about, this nature stuff."

"I'm going to gather coconuts with Julie and Willie. Come with me, you two. I wonder which one of you can find the most coconuts? Ready, set, go!" I knew making things feel like a game would help them. By the smiles on their faces, I think it's working.

Once we have pile of coconuts and a pile of wood I know we can finally rest for a little while. The kids are taking small sips of the last of their water, and I split the granola bar among the group. It's not much, but it's something. What we really need to do is open a coconut so we'll have more to drink.

This isn't easy like people make it look in the movies. After several tries at cracking it open nothing is working. Then I remember the video I watched one night. The man in the video said to find a sharp edge of a rock. Hold the coconut so the line is perpendicular to the sharp edge. After finding the best rock and following the instructions, the coconut breaks wide open. Some of the liquid spills on my shorts before I can lift it over my head, tilt it back, and drink. But I got some. Not bad for my first try.

Next time I'll be faster and save more of coconut juice into our empty water bottles. Breaking apart the coconut, I give everyone a piece to chew on.

"Something in our bellies is better than nothing, right?" I say to the group.

All anyone hears is teeth gnawing on the coconut until a sudden high-pitched far-off noise that sounds like a dying animal stops us all in our tracks. Suddenly the faces of all the children show worry. Even I can't hide it as Rory speaks first.

"Shh. It's okay everyone. Let's huddle closer to the fire," she suggests.

Just as we get closer together and calm starts to settle in, I notice the sky growing dark. Are those clouds coming our way? Will our fire make it through the night? At first I didn't want the rain, but then I remember something more important than wanting to stay warm and dry.

Water. We need water. Please let that storm come this way. We sit silently, nervously eating our coconut. We jump when we see lightning over the ocean, then hear a rumble in the distance. It's coming closer.

"Rory, you know what that storm means?" I ask, trying to sound upbeat and show some excitement.

"Sure do, Tyler. Let's get our bottles ready. You guys stay here." Rory jumps to her feet.

We collect every bottle and empty container we have and use large leaves as funnels so we'll catch as much rain as possible, even if the storm moves by quickly. Just as we have everything ready, the first drops hit my face. I look to the sky and feel another drop. It feels cool, and the thought of having full bottles of water to drink again is exciting.

The storm lasts a long time, and I know the fire won't continue. But that's all right. I can start it again. We pull some twigs and branches underneath us so they'll stay dry. Getting comfortable is not that easy, but somehow the younger kids fall asleep. They are curled up side by side, all snoring.

Rory and I can't seem to sleep though, even after I started the fire again.

"It must be so cool to have a dad like yours," I say to Rory, thinking about all of her dad's books.

"I guess so. I mean if you like that sort of thing. All I ever wanted was to be like every other kid," Rory says with a big sigh. "I wanted to play sports, not fly off to see the Grand Canyon, Niagara Falls, or the Sahara Desert. I've even been to the Taj Mahal, but I've never been in a soccer game with a bunch of friends."

"I would love to explore all those places," I say, but she looks kind of sad. "I can't imagine what it would be like if I had those adventures. I have loads of friends, and it's not that great."

Rory is laughing, and I'm not sure why. "Tyler, you are my first real friend, and I had to meet you on a shipwreck. That is pretty sad. We travel so much it's hard to make friends, so I just read my books and take pictures."

"I'd like to see your pictures sometime," I say, trying to get comfortable enough to sleep in the sand. "After this trip my mom will never let me go anywhere again. You'll have to email those pictures so I can pretend I'm with you on your next trip."

"You think we will have another trip? We'll be found?" Rory is biting her fingernails now, and I can tell she's scared.

"I know we will. We're doing everything right. Our parents are looking for us, and we're going to make it as easy as possible for them to find us."

"We need to do more tomorrow. A better shelter for the little kids."

"Then we better get some sleep." I lie down and roll toward the fire. Something about a fire always makes me sleepy.

"Goodnight, Tyler," Rory says as she yawns.

"Good night, Rory."

END OF CHAPTER 3 STATS

<u>Achievement:</u> 3866 words! (more than half way done)

<u>Characters:</u>
   Tyler - Making the fire
   Rory - SOS sign
   Tom - Gets hurt
   Willie - Collecting coconuts
   Julie - Full of energy

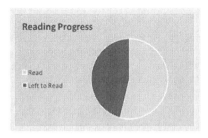

CHAPTER 4

I t's time to go in the jungle. I know it's important, but the rest
of the group seems to think we should stay put and not move.
I feel something quickly crawl across my foot, and I kick it across
the sand. A huge crab is clamping its pinchers in my direction.
That little crab is the least of our worries. There are way more
dangerous things here.

Maybe if I was six like Julie I wouldn't worry, because I'd have
no idea how bad this is.

We gather all the coconuts from the edges of the jungle. It
won't be enough to feed us for long. There is no sign of rain so we
can't count on that for more fresh water.

It's time to be brave. Go in farther to get more food and look
around. It hasn't rained for a couple days, and we need fresh
water. We need food. I went fishing but had no luck. Why did I
think fishing with my granddad last summer would be enough of
a lesson? We had poles and bait, but really granddad did most of
the work. This is totally different. I try to use a stick I'd sharpened
into a spear, but the fish are way too fast.

I remember one summer we were driving through the smallest
state in the United States, Rhode Island, and saw men in the water

with rakes. My mom told me they were gathering quahogs. They are like clams. So I decide to try. I remember you need to wait until it's low tide.

I have the group help me make a rake out of our gear and some sticks. When we find some clams, Rory tells me they are called cockles here, and they are good to eat. If we steam them, they will open. It's hard to do over the fire, but we are finally able to. The problem is they are slimy and the little kids don't like them. We need other kinds of food that they'll eat to stay strong and healthy.

"Rory, are you ready to do more searching?" I ask as I tighten the laces on my sneakers.

"Do you think we really need to go in there?" Rory asks, folding her arms over her chest.

"That's where the food and water will be," I remind her. "We'll run out of food and water here on the shore."

Rory and I jump when we hear a weird noise that sounds like someone throwing up. It sounds like that because it is. Willie is sick.

"Willie are you okay?" I ask, feeling queasy when I see him throwing up. Willie struggles to respond as he bends over and holds his stomach.

Rory looks way better than I do as she goes over to him. "We need to help him," she says sitting close by him. "Willie everything is going to be all right."

"What's wrong with him?" Julie asks, starting to cry. "Are we all going to be sick?"

"I think he might be dehydrated," Rory says to me quietly. "Look at him. He seems really tired and his lips are so dry. Those are signs."

"We need to find more water," I say, relieved that Willie is sitting up and looking like he's at least not going to be sick anymore.

Rory looks like she's not bothered by it at all. "Willie, we're going to find you some water, and you'll feel better."

"Let's get him in the shade. Julie, I need you to make a fan out of those big leaves. Can you try and cool off Willie?" I ask, not looking at Willie's mess in the sand.

Willie tries to stand, but he is unsteady. It's clear he's dizzy, and Rory is right. He's showing all the signs of dehydration. But how can that be? He's gotten as much to drink as the rest of us, and we're all fine.

"Yes, I think I can do that," Julie answers with a nervous sound in her voice. "Is he going to be all right?"

"Yes," Rory says firmly.

"He's been drinking as much as us, hasn't he?" I ask, scratching my head. "We have to go get more water."

"But there's an ocean of water right there, Tyler," Willie mumbles, and his lips look really dry.

"We can't drink that, Willie, remember? It's not safe for us," Rory says, keeping her voice soft and kind.

Willie doesn't answer, and my stomach starts to ache thinking about what might have happened.

"Willie, did you drink the ocean water?" Rory asks, still sounding nice.

"Mm hmm," he answers, nodding just a little.

"We need to get him some fresh water right away. It will help flush out the ocean water he drank. I will stay with him though, not Julie. He'll need someone to watch him closely," Rory decides, and since she seems to know the most about this I agree with her.

"Tom and Julie, let's go. We'll go into the jungle together and find something to help. Grab the empty bottles."

"I'm scared," Tommy says, and I want to tell him I am too. He hangs on my arm, and it's making it tough to move. As we enter the jungle I realize the trees and vines are so thick it'll be hard to move with these little kids. But if Willie gets worse I don't want them to have to see that.

"It's okay, Tommy. We'll get through this. Just think of the great adventure you can tell all your friends when you get home. You're on an island. You're taking care of yourself and helping your friend. You can be a hero."

"This trip was my dad's idea. I just want to go home and color," Tommy moans. "I like to color and read my books."

"You'll be back home doing that soon," I say, but he's not moving any faster. "We can't go anywhere until we find what we need. What Willie needs."

Up ahead I see something and feel better right away. I know that tree, and I know it will help us all.

"Julie, those trees ahead, do you know what they are?" I ask, pointing to my left so she can see.

"Yes! They are bananas. I love bananas," Julie answers, excitedly pointing at the yellow fruit and jumping up and down. Even Tommy seems excited.

"Okay, let's check those out and see what we can find. Maybe we can get some bananas. I bet that will help Willie."

There are monkeys in the trees, and they are making noises that clearly tell us they aren't going to share their bananas. I can only snatch a couple of bunches, but it's better than nothing.

"What's that?" Tommy asks. "It sounds like the faucet running when my mom fills the tub for me."

I toss the bananas down to them and climb down, away from the monkeys. I stop to listen and realize he's right. I hear running water too.

"Julie, listen," I say, cupping a hand to my ear, and she does the same.

"We need to get to that water, Tyler," Tommy says, finally looking energized.

We head deeper into the jungle. If I thought the terrain was difficult before, I was wrong. This is thicker and the vines and picky bushes are making my skin sting. But we need to push through.

"Just up here, guys. I can see it clearing," I tell the other two. I can see it now. The waterfall. It's beautiful. I smell clean fresh water. I know how much this water is needed. This is what will help us survive.

Just then a loud high-pitched scream makes me freeze. It's Julie. I open my eyes and feel it. There is something smooth on my neck, and it's tracking down my arm. Within seconds I'm running and tossing a long yellow snake off me. I hate snakes. But Willie needs this water, and I have to keep going. I lean down, my hands shaking, and fill the bottles.

END OF CHAPTER 4 STATS

Achievement: 5293 words! (more than half way done)

Characters:
    Tyler - Climbs a tree
    Rory - Stays with Willie
    Tom - Hears the waterfall
    Willie - Drank salt water
    Julie - Screams

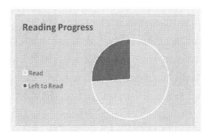

CHAPTER FIVE

I can see our camp ahead. I'm happy we have water for Willie to feel better, but I can't stop thinking about that snake. It feels like something is still crawling on me.

"I can't believe you grabbed that snake and threw it off of you, Tyler," Rory says after hearing the story from Julie. It almost sounds like she is upset she missed out on the latest adventure.

"I wasn't really thinking about it. I knew we needed to get to that water, and my adrenaline was pumping, I guess. Julie's scream told me something bad was happening. So I have her to thank."

"Was she the only one who screamed?" Rory laughs.

"We know where the water is. It's an easy walk now that we've made a little path. There's plenty of water for all of us. We'll just have to watch out for the snakes. With that crossed off the list, it's time to make this shelter better," I tell them, trying to get them to forget about me yelling and running away from a snake.

"Willie, are you feeling better?" Rory asks, and I'm glad she's here to help.

"I think so. The water is helping." Willie sits up and looks better.

"Take a while longer before you try and do too much," Rory tells him and helps him lie back down.

"Rory, can you help me gather some better vines and those large leaves over there? These palm pieces are good. We already have a start on the floor to keep us out of the sand. Now we need some cover for a roof. This way we won't get soaked when it rains again, and we will have some shade during the day."

I start building a triangle shape around the floor we made. It's beginning to look like a tepee. I made these in the backyard and on a couple camping trips. I'm good at this. I put Tommy on my shoulders, and we walk around in circles while Tommy wraps the vines around the top to give it a little extra strength. We are becoming a good team.

"I'll layer the smaller branches and cover the holes," Rory says. "When I'm done we'll start adding these large leaves on top. It's starting to look like a real shelter now."

Finally feeling good about the shelter, I think about ways to get us noticed. I know we need to make smoke and lots of it. I remember this show about needing damp leaves. I don't want to put out our fire; it helps us stay warm and cook. So I think about making a few other fires farther down the beach. We don't want to smell the smoke; we just want it to catch the attention of any passing boats or planes.

"Rory, we need to get some wet leaves and twigs. That will help us make smoke. It's time to think about being rescued, not just surviving. I'm going to start two new fires and use them to make smoke," I say, dusting the sand off my hands.

Rory nods. "I'll gather some. Tommy, come with me and we'll get what we need while Tyler builds the new fires. Build them near the SOS sign in the sand that Julie and I worked on."

After a short time I have one of the fires going, and it's raging.

Willie seems to be doing better. I ask him to dig a hole in the sand to put the leaves and twigs in to keep them damp. It's a small job and he seems up to it. Hopefully he learned his lesson about drinking ocean water, no matter how thirsty he is.

"I have one of the fires going, guys. Let's use this one and see what kind of smoke we can make." Everyone grabs handfuls of damp leaves and starts to pile them on. At first I think it will smother the fire, but it actually starts to work.

Billows of white smoke rise from the fire. I know we need more, but it's a good start. I finish the second fire and make a plan to keep them going. We head back to our shelter, and the two big fires continue burning. I can see the smoke from our camp. I only hope someone else will too. Someone who can rescue us. I hand out peeled bananas and water we boiled.

"We need to think about more food now. We have water, shelter, and a couple things to eat. We have a rescue plan in place with the smoke and the SOS sign in the sand. We need more bananas. The monkeys must move on now and then."

Julie smiles. "They are cute."

"Not when they want the bananas we need," I say seriously.

Tommy, who has been listening to my advice and lessons, speaks up. "We could be here a while, so we need to start thinking long term. Maybe we should make our shelter up in the trees like the monkeys. I'm sure it's safer up there. We can figure out a way to scare them off and take their bananas."

I hear a sniffle and then someone crying. I expect it to be one of the younger kids, but it's Rory and she's running off.

"Rory, come back! It's not safe out there alone," I yell to her, but she doesn't stop. She's out of the firelight, and I've lost her.

END OF CHAPTER 5 STATS

<u>Achievement:</u> 6,268 words!

<u>Characters:</u>
   Tyler - Still feels the snake
   Rory - Feeling sad
   Tom - Ready to help
   Willie - Getting Better
   Julie - Likes the monkeys

CHAPTER 6

"Rory, wait up. Wait for me. Please!" I try to get her to stop, but she is much faster than I am. I finally catch up to her when she stops and leans against a tree. It doesn't look like she's tired or hurt. She probably felt bad for me.

"Tyler, I'm getting scared that we will never get home. I know you agree with Tommy. If you want us all moving farther into the jungle, it means you don't think we are ever getting out of here. We aren't going home." She sounds very scared, and her voice is shaking.

"I'm sorry, Rory. I think we may want to make a better shelter, but not because we're stuck here forever. I know someone will come for us. It's just a matter of time." I say that to her confidently, but somewhere deep inside I'm not sure if I believe it. We don't know where we are. The island is very small and the part of the ocean we were traveling through is vast and hard to navigate. If we are going to be here a little longer, we have to do everything we can to stay alive. "I just want to make sure we're being as safe as possible until the rescuers find us."

"I don't know if I believe you," she says with a shrug. "I like my math teacher, and she'd tell me the odds. What are the odds we'll be found?"

"I'm terrible at math," I joke. "I don't know anything about how to figure our odds of getting home. But I know my mom. And there is no one better at this stuff than your dad. So forget what the numbers say, and let's just remember how lucky we are to have made it this far. I know if we keep doing all the things we have been doing, someone will find us."

"I know I sound like a baby, but I want to go home," she says, sniffling again.

"Then we are both babies because all I want to do is see my mother again. Play in my room. Shoot some baskets at the park. I know this isn't easy, but as the two oldest kids here, it's important for us to take care of the younger ones. We need to keep them safe for as long as possible instead of lying there hoping and dreaming we will be rescued. You know more about all of this than I do. You're faster. You're strong. I can't do this without you."

I know Rory is hearing me. She wipes the tears from her eyes and stands a little straighter. She knows what I'm saying is true. "I'm not stronger than you," she argues.

"In a lot of ways you are," I reply. "We just need to keep going."

"My dad would say the same thing." She looks at the sand and kicks it around a little with her feet.

"I know my mom won't stop searching for us. They are probably getting closer every day. Knowing how good your dad is at survival, he probably already has all the parents who were on the other life raft rescued and is putting together a plan to find us."

I look at the sky, hoping to get answers. Like magically someone will drop down from there and help us. I don't get much except a bit of an empty feeling. The world feels very big right now. Then I see it. A shooting star.

"Did you see that Rory?" I know she didn't because she was looking at the ground. But she follows my eyes and looks up to the sky with me.

"There's another one," I say, pointing to the shooting star.

"A wishing star," Rory says, and her eyes open wide, looking at the sparkling stars.

"Let's wait for the next one and make a wish together. Maybe if we both make the same wish at the exact same time, it will be much more powerful." I know I sound like a little kid right now, but I don't care. I'll try anything. Even magic.

"Sounds like a plan, Tyler," Rory laughs.

As the next shooting star shoots across the sky, we close our eyes and wish for someone to come get us. Soon!

END OF CHAPTER 6 STATS

Achievement: 7,029 words!

Characters:
    Tyler - Makes a wish
    Rory - Runs away

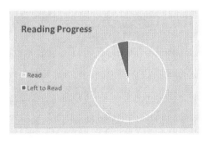

CHAPTER 7

R ory is in charge of keeping track of what day it is. She uses a sharp rock she found and makes a check on a large piece of bark. By the look of it we have been here for two weeks. It started off difficult and bumpy. But working together seems like we've made it. We have the fires going every day for the smoke. We have a great system for making sure they have wet leaves on them all the time.

Willie is the best at remembering it. He knows how to wet the leaves and twigs before placing them on the fire, and that helps to create nice white smoke.

The shelter is better than it was. We still have the tepee for sleeping at night, but I usually stay by the fire. I know they feel safer together inside.

The food is better too. After a few tries of different methods, we figured out the best way to catch fish with a spear. That's been the coolest part so far. Julie is really good at it because she's so small and makes the least amount of waves when she moves around the shallow water. Although when she catches one, she makes me take the fish away before she has to see it.

There is a small cove where the water is manageable in low

tide. It takes a while, but if I'm patient we can gather enough fish for us each day. I also found other ocean creatures that we've tried. We now spend the day playing in the fresh water by the waterfall to keep cool and clean.

"I bet I can do a handstand longer than you," Tommy shouts as he splashes around.

"Ready, set, go," Rory says as she times him. I close my eyes and pretend this is just a summer day at the pool in my backyard.

I let Tommy win the handstand contest. Keeping the younger kids happy works best. I'm surprised how much we've gotten used to this place. It's not home. We miss our parents. But we've made it a little better every day. Staying busy is important, and there is plenty to do. Rory keeps everyone organized, and Julie keeps us laughing.

As we splash in the fresh water under the falls, I keep my eyes open for snakes.

"Do you hear that?" Rory asks, quickly climbing out of the water. I do the same, knowing any sound could be a chance at rescue.

It gets louder and my heart starts to pound. Rory and I look at each other as we figure out the sound at the same time.

"HELICOPTER!" we yell and start running back toward the shore.

I hear the patter of feet not that far behind me.

"Willie, get to it. The fires need smoke," I yell. He passes me and runs toward one of the fires as I run to the other.

He's grabbing the damp leaves and twigs and putting them on top of the fire. The smoke rises, but we need more. "Tommy, Julie, and Rory: get whatever you can. Get the whistles from my kit and start blowing them like crazy."

Everyone is doing their job, and I feel proud. I can hear the helicopter, but we haven't seen it yet. The smoke is as heavy and high as we've ever had it. If the helicopter is close by, someone on board will have to see us.

I see Rory run to the SOS sign she made in the sand.

She yells to us in between blowing on her whistle. "Everyone start waving your hands in the air. Try to get noticed."

I'm pretty sure it would be impossible to hear the whistles over the loud whoosh of helicopter blades, but I'm glad they're trying.

Finally, the helicopter flies over. It looks like it's going to fly right past us. We turn to see the back end of the copter start to bank left.

"It's coming back" I yell, my throat sore from the smoke and screaming. They are trying to find a place to land.

As the helicopter lands and the door opens, I see someone I recognize. It's not my family, but it's Rory's dad. I recognize his picture from the back of all his books.

"Dad!" Rory yells and runs toward him. He is running out of the helicopter just as fast. They meet in the middle, and he picks her up and spins her around.

"Let's go, guys. This is it. We're rescued," I say. We all hold hands and run toward the helicopter together. Rory's dad puts her down and kneels in the sand. He opens his arms wide and the three younger kids run into them. I stand back for a second and realize we are going home. I can't wait to see my mother.

The helicopter turns off its engine, and we can hear again. "I'm so glad I found you kids. This has been one heck of an adventure. Let's get you home. All your parents are safe and sound, waiting for you. They had an adventure of their own on their lifeboat," he says to us, looking over his shoulder at the things we've done to get attention. "But it seems like you were just as prepared. I can't believe you did all this yourselves.

"Just us kids." Rory smiles.

We hop on the helicopter, and I'm so excited for the ride. It takes longer than I hoped, since I'm anxious to see my mom.

I can see the dirt landing strip ahead. I can see a large gathering of people off to the side as I look out my window. It looks like everyone is either cheering, crying, or waving. The younger kids are so excited to see their parents that they are all crying as well. Somewhere inside, I'm kind of sad to see our adventure end. I'm also very happy to be going home.

"Dad, I think I'm done with this adventure thing. I've had more adventure in a few weeks than I'd like to have in a lifetime," Rory says to her father.

"Rory, you can have whatever you want," he promises. "I've been having my way long enough. I was so worried about you. I'm ready to do things however you want now."

"I know what I want, Dad. I want to move to wherever Tyler lives. I want to live in his town and be normal."

I lean over and interrupt. "I'm not sure, after this, any of us will ever be normal again."

The End

END OF CHAPTER 7 STATS

Achievement: 8,312 words!

Characters:
    Tyler - Catching Fish
    Rory - In charge of the date
    Tom - Handstand contest
    Willie - Make the fire smoke
    Julie -Best at fishing

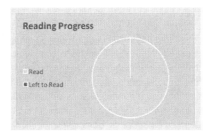

I hope you have enjoyed this exciting adventure! *Just Us Kids* will be a series of books filled with heroes in all sorts of different environments. Stay tuned for thrilling new books!

Made in the USA
Monee, IL
27 November 2021

83066383R00035